Go Eat Worms

"The worms are going to get revenge, Todd," Regina said. "They saw what you did. Now they're planning their revenge."

Todd let out a scornful laugh. "You must think I'm as stupid as you are!" he declared. "There's no way I'm going to fall for that. No way I'm going to believe such a stupid idea."

Giggling to each other, Regina and Beth returned to their ping-pong game.

Todd dropped the two worm halves into the tank. To his surprise, four more worms had poked up out of the soft dirt. They were staring straight up at him.

Todd stared down at them, thinking about what Regina and Beth had said.

What a stupid idea, he thought. Those worms weren't watching me.

Or *were* they?

Go Eat Worms

R.L. Stine

Hippo

Scholastic Children's Books,
Commonwealth House, 1-19 New Oxford Street,
London, WC1A 1NU, UK
a division of Scholastic Publications Ltd
London ~ New York ~ Toronto ~ Sydney ~ Auckland

First published in the US by Scholastic Inc., 1994
First published in the UK by Scholastic Ltd, 1995

ISBN: 0 590 55929 X

Printed by Cox & Wyman Ltd, Reading, Berks
Typeset by Contour Typesetters, Southall, London

10 9 8

Before the worms turned mean, before they slithered out to get their revenge, Todd Barstow had a great time with them.

Todd collected worms. He built a worm farm in his basement.

He studied them. He played with them. He did experiments with them. Sometimes he carried them around with him.

Sometimes he scared people with them. Especially his sister, Regina.

He liked to dangle the long, purple ones in front of Regina's face. Sometimes he dropped them down her back or into her long, brown hair.

He liked to torture Regina's best friend, too. Her name was Beth Baker, and she always screamed a high, squeaky scream whenever Todd surprised her with a big, slimy worm.

"You're disgusting, Todd!" Beth would squeal.

This always made Todd very happy.

1

Todd's best friend, Danny Fletcher, didn't really understand why Todd was so interested in worms. But Danny *did* understand how much fun it was to surprise people and make them scream. So he spent a lot of time with Todd.

In fact, the two of them were almost always together. They even sat together in Miss Grant's class, where they whispered a lot, planning what to do next with Todd's worms.

Todd didn't look at all mischievous. In fact, he usually had a very serious expression on his face. He had dark brown eyes under short, wavy brown hair. No one ever saw his hair. It was always covered by the silver-and-black Raiders cap he wore day and night.

He was tall and skinny. His mother said he was as skinny as a worm. Todd never thought that was funny. He took worms seriously.

Danny looked more like a joker. He had a round, chubby face under curly red hair, and a really goofy grin. His round blue eyes always lit up when Todd was about to spring a big, wet worm on an unsuspecting victim.

Whenever Todd succeeded in making someone scream in surprise, Danny would toss back his head, let out a high-pitched cheer, and slap Todd hard on the back with his chubby, freckled hand. Then the two of them would screech with laughter, roll around on the floor, and enjoy their victory.

2

They had a great time with worms.

But whenever anyone asked Todd why he collected them, and why he was so interested in them, Todd's expression would turn serious, and he'd say, "Because I want to be a scientist when I grow up."

"How many worms do you have?" someone asked him.

"Not enough," he replied.

He was always digging up more. Looking for champions. He liked them long and purple and kind of fat.

And squishy. Squishy was very important.

Sunday night it had rained. The ground was still wet as Todd and Regina walked to school on Monday morning. Todd knew the worms would all be coming up for air.

He found Danny at the water fountain outside their classroom. Danny had a finger pressed over the fountain spout, and when kids passed by, he made the water squirt all over them.

Todd lowered his Raiders cap over his forehead as he leaned close to Danny. "Meet me behind second base in the playground," he whispered. "As soon as the lunch bell rings."

Danny nodded. He didn't have to ask why. He knew that Todd's favourite place to dig up fresh worms was the bare patch of ground behind second base on the softball diamond.

The ground there was soft and rich. And after a good rain, the two boys could shovel up ten to fifteen worms without even trying.

Todd kept a gardening shovel in his locker, as well as a small metal bucket with a lid. He was always ready to collect worms when the time was right.

In class that morning, everyone was talking about the big Science Expo to be held in the gym on Saturday. Some kids already had their projects done.

Debby Brewster was bragging about how she was going to win the new computer, the grand prize, by making electricity. Someone shouted out, "Go fly a kite!" and everyone laughed. The whole class was tired of Debby's constant bragging.

Todd's project was just about finished. It had worms in it, of course.

It was a worm house. A little house Todd's father had helped him build, about the size of a doll's house. One side was cut away and covered with a pane of glass so you could see in. The house was filled with dirt. And you could see all of the worms—a whole worm family—crawling from room to room.

Danny's project was really boring. He was building the solar system out of balloons.

He wanted to share Todd's project and work

4

on it with him. But Todd wouldn't let him. "I don't want to share the computer," Todd had said.

"But I helped you dig up the worms!" Danny protested.

"I dug up most of them," Todd replied.

And so Todd forced Danny to do his own project. Danny blew up different-coloured balloons for all the planets and taped them on a big black sheet of card.

Very boring.

"What makes you so sure you're going to win the grand prize?" Danny asked Todd as he hurried to catch up with him in the playground at lunchtime.

"I had a look at the other projects," Todd replied. "My project is the only one with real, living creatures. Except for Heather's snails."

"Heather has done a lot of experiments with her snails," Danny commented.

"So what?" Todd snapped. "Snails are for babies. We had snails in first grade. No one cares about snails in *sixth* grade. No way they can compete with worms."

"I guess you're right," Danny replied, scratching his red hair.

They squatted down as they reached the bare spot behind second base. Todd handed Danny his spare shovel.

5

The playground was empty. Everyone else was inside eating lunch.

The ground was still soft and wet. Worms were poking their heads up from little puddles. One long worm crawled on top of the dirt.

"The rain makes them all come up," said Todd, beginning to dig. "This is excellent!"

He didn't know what kind of trouble was waiting under the ground.

"Look out. You cut that one in two," Todd warned.

Danny grinned. "So what? Now you've got two little ones."

"But I only like big ones," Todd replied, carefully sliding his shovel under a long, fat worm.

"How many more do you need? My stomach is growling," Danny complained, glancing back at the long, redbrick school building.

"Just a few more," Todd said, lowering the fat worm into the bucket. "He's a squirmer, isn't he?"

Danny groaned. "Everyone else is eating lunch, and I'm out here digging in the mud."

"It's for science," Todd said seriously.

"This one is as big as a snake. Did you ever think of collecting snakes?" Danny asked.

"No," Todd replied quickly, digging deep into the mud. "No way."

7

"Why not?"

"Because I like worms," Todd said.

"What's the *real* reason?" Danny demanded.

"My parents won't let me," Todd muttered.

The two boys continued to dig for another few minutes until the ground started to rumble. Danny dropped his shovel.

"What's that?" he asked.

"Huh?" Todd didn't seem to notice.

The ground rumbled a little harder. This time everything shook.

Todd pitched forward, dropping on to his hands and knees. He gazed up at Danny, surprised. "Hey—don't push me."

"I didn't!" Danny protested.

"Then what—?" Todd started. But the ground shook again. And the dirt made a soft cracking sound.

"I—I don't like this!" Danny stammered.

Without another word, both boys started to run.

But the ground trembled again, and the cracking sound beneath their trainers grew louder. Closer.

"Earthquake!" Todd screamed. "Earthquake!"

Todd and Danny sprinted across the field and the playground and burst into the lunchroom.

Both boys had red faces. Both of them were breathing hard.

"Earthquake!" Todd shouted. "It's an earthquake!"

Chairs scraped. Conversations stopped. Everyone turned to stare at the two of them.

"Duck under the tables!" Danny screamed shrilly. "Quick, everyone! The ground is shaking!"

"Earthquake! Earthquake!"

Everyone just laughed.

No one moved.

No one wanted to fall for a stupid practical joke.

Todd spotted Beth and Regina across the lunchroom at the window. He and Danny darted over to them.

"Get away from the window!" Todd warned.

"The ground is cracking apart!" Danny cried.

Regina's mouth dropped open. She didn't know whether to believe them or not. Regina, the worrier, was always ready to believe a disaster waited just around the corner.

But all the other kids in the huge lunchroom were laughing their heads off.

"We don't get earthquakes in Ohio," Beth said simply, making a disgusted face at Todd.

"But—but—but—" Todd sputtered.

"Didn't you feel it?" Danny demanded breathlessly, his round, chubby face still bright red. "Didn't you feel the ground shake?"

"We didn't feel anything," Beth replied.

"Didn't you *hear* it?" Todd cried. "I—I was so freaked, I dropped all my worms." He sank into the chair next to his sister.

"No one believes you. It's a stupid joke, Todd," Regina told him. "Better luck next time."

"But—but—"

Regina turned away from her sputtering brother and started talking to Beth again. "As I was saying, his head is way too big for his body."

"He looks okay to me," Beth replied.

"No. We'll have to cut his head off," Regina insisted, frowning into her bowl of noodle soup.

"Major surgery?" Beth asked. "Are you sure? If we cut his head off, it'll show. It really will."

"But if his head is too big, what choice do we have?" Regina whined.

"Huh? What are you talking about?" Todd demanded. "What about the earthquake?"

"Todd, we're talking about our science fair project," Beth said impatiently.

"Yeah. Go out and play in the earthquake!" Regina snapped. "We've got problems with Christopher Robin."

Todd sniggered. "What a stupid name for a bird."

Regina stuck out her tongue at him and then turned her back. She and Beth began discussing their project again.

They both agreed they probably should have tried something a little easier. And smaller.

They were building an enormous robin out of papier-mâché. It was supposed to be lifelike in every detail, except size.

But the girls quickly discovered that papier-mâché isn't the most lifelike material around. It was hard to get the wings to stick to the body. It was even harder to get the huge round body to stand on the spindly wooden legs.

And now Regina was convinced that the bird's head was much too big for its body.

They had used an entire quart of orange paint on the bird's chest. Now, if they had to cut the head off and make a new one, the paint job would be ruined!

"Maybe we could just shave a little off the top," Beth suggested, taking the last crisp from her bag and crinkling the bag between her hands. "Can I have some of your soup?"

"You can finish it," Regina replied, sliding the bowl across the table. "I'm not very hungry."

"There's going to be an aftershock," Todd warned, staring out of the window.

"Yeah. There's always an aftershock after an earthquake," Danny agreed.

"I can't believe you're sitting here calmly, talking about your stupid project," Todd said.

"It's not a stupid project!" Beth replied angrily.

"Todd, go eat worms!" Regina exclaimed. It was her favourite thing to say to her brother. She said it at least ten times a day.

"Beth is already eating worms," Todd said, gazing down at the bowl of soup.

Danny laughed.

"Give me a break, Todd," Beth muttered, rolling her eyes.

"No. Really," Todd insisted. "What kind of soup is that?"

"Chicken noodle," Beth replied warily. She took a spoonful, slurping the soup off the spoon.

"Well, there's a worm in your soup," Todd said with a serious face.

"Todd, you're not funny," Beth replied. "Give up."

"Want to bet?" Todd challenged.

"Bet? What do you mean 'bet'?" Beth said.

"I'll bet you a dollar there's a worm in your soup," Todd told her, his dark eyes lighting up.

Danny leaned across the table, a wide grin frozen on his chubby face. "Yummm," he said, licking his lips. "A big fat purple one! Can I have a taste?"

"You two are pathetic," Regina muttered.

"Bet a dollar?" Todd challenged, ignoring his sister.

"Sure. It's a bet," Beth said.

She reached across the table and shook Todd's hand to seal the bet. Then she ran the soup spoon through the bowl several times to show him there was no worm.

Todd reached under the table. Then a smile crossed his face as he brought his hand up—and dropped a fat purple worm into Beth's soup.

The worm wriggled and squirmed as it hit the hot soup.

"Oooh, yuk!" Beth screamed.

Danny let out a loud laugh and slapped Todd gleefully on the back, nearly knocking Todd off the chair.

"Pay up, Beth," Todd demanded. "You lost the bet."

"You guys are sick," Regina murmured, making a disgusted face, forcing herself not to look into the soup bowl.

"Yuck! Disgusting!" Beth was shrieking.

The worm slipped and swam through the noodles.

"You said you dropped your worms outside," Regina accused angrily.

Todd shrugged, a big grin on his face. "I lied!"

Danny laughed even harder. He pounded the table gleefully with his fists, making the soup bowl bounce up and down.

"Hey!" Suddenly Todd's smile faded. He stared out of the lunchroom window at the playground.

"Look!" He hit Danny's shoulder, then pointed out towards second base, to the bare spot behind the base. "What's going on out there?" he cried.

14

Todd walked over to the window and peered out, pressing his nose against the glass. "What is Patrick MacKay doing in my worm-digging spot?" he demanded angrily.

Danny stepped beside Todd. He squinted out into the grey afternoon. "Are you sure that's Patrick MacKay?"

The sky darkened as the low clouds gathered. The boy on the playground was half covered by shadow. But Todd recognized him anyway.

That snobby, stuck-up, rich kid. Patrick MacKay.

He was bent over the bare spot of mud behind second base, working feverishly.

"What is he *doing* out there?" Todd repeated. "That's my best worm spot!"

"He's digging up worms, too!" Regina declared from the table.

"Huh?" Todd spun round to find his sister smirking at him.

15

"Patrick is digging up worms for the Science Expo," she told him, unable to hide her joy. "He's doing a worm project, too."

"But he *can't!*" Todd sputtered in a high, shrill voice.

"Whoa! What a copycat!" Danny declared.

"He can't do a worm project! *I'm* doing the worm project!" Todd insisted, turning back to stare at Patrick through the glass.

"It's a free country," Regina replied smugly. She and Beth laughed. They were enjoying seeing Todd squirm for a change.

"But he's not into worms!" Todd continued, very upset. "He doesn't collect worms! He doesn't study worms! He's just copying me!"

"Look at him, digging in your spot," Danny murmured, shaking his head bitterly.

"Patrick is a nice guy," Beth remarked. "He doesn't act like an idiot and put worms in people's soup."

"He's an idiot," Todd insisted angrily, staring hard out of the window. "He's a total idiot."

"He's a copycat idiot," Danny added.

"His worm project is going to be better than yours," Regina teased him.

Todd's dark eyes burned into his sister's. "You know what it is? You know what Patrick's project is?"

Regina had a smug smile on her lips. She tossed back her brown hair. Then she made a

16

zipper sign, moving her fingers across her lips.

"I'll never tell," she said.

"What is it?" Todd demanded. "Tell me."

Regina shook her head.

"Tell me, Beth," Todd insisted, narrowing his eyes menacingly at her.

"No way," Beth replied, glancing merrily at Regina.

"Then I'll ask him myself," Todd declared. "Come on, Danny."

The two boys started running through the lunchroom. They were nearly at the door when Todd ran into their teacher.

Miss Grant was carrying her lunch tray high over her head, stepping round a group of kids in the aisle. Todd just didn't see her.

He bumped her from behind.

She uttered a cry of surprise—and her tray flew out of her hands. The tray and the plates clattered loudly on to the floor. And her food—salad and a bowl of spaghetti—dropped around her feet.

"What is your hurry, young man?" she snapped at Todd.

"Uh . . . sorry," Todd murmured. It was the only reply he could think of.

Miss Grant bent to examine her brown shoes, which were now orange, covered with wet clumps of spaghetti.

"It was an accident," Todd said impatiently,

fiddling with his Raiders cap.

"It certainly was," the teacher replied coldly. "Perhaps I should speak to you after school about why we don't run in the lunchroom?"

"Perhaps," Todd agreed. Then he bolted past her, running through the door faster than he had ever run.

"Well done, Todd!" Danny exclaimed, running beside him.

"It wasn't my fault," Todd told him. "She stepped in front of me."

"The bell is going to ring," Danny warned as they made their way out of the back door.

"I don't care," Todd replied breathlessly. "I've got to find out what that copycat is doing with worms!"

Patrick was still bent over the mud behind second base. He was scooping up worms with a silvery towel that looked brand-new, then dropping them into a metal bait can.

He was a slim, good-looking boy with wavy blond hair and blue eyes. He had started school in September. His family had moved to Ohio from Pasadena. He was always telling everyone how California was so much better.

He didn't brag about how rich he was. But he wore designer jeans, and his mother brought him to school every morning in a long, white Lincoln. So Todd and the others at William

Tecumseh Sherman Middle School worked it out.

Patrick was in Regina's class. A few weeks after school started, he'd had a big birthday party and invited everyone in his class. Including Regina.

She reported that Patrick had a whole funfair, with rides and everything, in his back garden. Todd pretended he didn't care that he wasn't invited.

The sky grew even darker as Danny and Todd stood over Patrick in the playground. "What are you doing, Patrick?" Todd demanded.

"Digging," Patrick replied, glancing up from his work.

"Digging up worms?" Todd asked, his hands pressed against the waist of his jeans.

Patrick nodded. He started digging again. He pulled up a long, dark brown one that Todd would have loved to own.

"*I'm* doing a worm project," Todd told him.

"I know," Patrick replied, concentrating on his work. "Me, too."

"What is it?" Danny chimed in. "What's your project, Patrick?"

Patrick didn't reply. He dug up a tiny, pale worm, examined it, and tossed it back.

"What's your project? Tell us," Todd demanded.

"You really want to know?" Patrick asked,

19

raising his blue eyes to them. The wind ruffled his blond hair, but the hair immediately fell back into place.

Todd felt a raindrop on his shoulder. Then one on the top of his head.

"What's your project?" Todd repeated.

"Okay, okay," Patrick said, wiping dirt off his hands. "I'll tell you. My project is . . ."

The class bell rang. The sharp clang cut through the rising wind. The rain started to patter loudly against the ground.

"We've got to go in," Danny urged, tugging at Todd's sleeve.

"Wait," Todd said, his eyes on Patrick. "Tell me now!" he insisted.

"But we'll be late!" Danny insisted, tugging at Todd again. "And we're getting soaked."

Patrick climbed to his feet. "I think I've got all the worms I need." He shook wet dirt off the silvery towel.

"So what is your worm project?" Todd repeated, ignoring the pattering rain and Danny's urgent requests to get back inside the school.

Patrick grinned at him, revealing about three hundred perfect, white teeth. "I'm teaching them to fly," he said.

"Huh?"

"I'm putting cardboard wings on them and

teaching them to fly. Wait till you see it! It's a riot!" He burst out laughing.

Danny leaned close to Todd. "Is he for real?" he whispered.

"Of course not!" Todd shot back. "Don't be an idiot, Danny. He's having us on."

"Hey—you're not funny," Danny told Patrick angrily.

"We're late, guys. Let's get going," Patrick said, his grin fading. He started towards the school building.

But Todd moved quickly to block his path. "Tell me the truth, Patrick. What are you planning to do?"

Patrick started to reply.

But a low rumbling sound made him stop.

They all heard it. A muffled roar that made the ground shake.

The worm can fell out of Patrick's hand. His blue eyes opened wide in surprise—and fear.

The rumbling gave way to a loud, cracking noise. It sounded as if the whole playground were splitting apart.

"Wh-what's *happening*?" Patrick stammered.

"Run!" Todd screamed as the ground trembled and shook. "Run for your life!"

"Why are you so late? Where've you been? In another earthquake?" Regina teased.

"Ha-ha," Todd said bitterly. "Danny and I weren't making it up. It happened again! And Patrick was there, too."

"How come no one else felt it?" Regina demanded. "I had the radio on after school. And there was nothing about an earthquake on the news."

It was nearly five o'clock. Todd had found his sister in the garage, up on an aluminium ladder, working hard on her giant robin. Somehow she had managed to get clumps of papier-mâché in her hair and down the front of her T-shirt.

"I don't want to talk about the earthquake," Todd muttered, stepping into the garage. "I know I'm right."

The rain had ended just before school finished. But the driveway was still puddled with water.

His wet trainers squeaked as he made his way to Regina's ladder.

"Where's Beth?" he asked.

"She had to go and get her brace tightened," Regina told him, concentrating on smoothing out the papier-mâché beak. She let out a loud groan. "I can't get this beak smooth."

Todd kicked dejectedly at an old tyre that was leaning against the garage wall.

"Look out!" Regina called.

A wet clump of papier-mâché landed at Todd's feet with a plop. "You missed me!" he cried, ducking away.

"So? Where've you been?" Regina asked.

"Miss Grant kept me after school. She gave me a long lecture."

"About what?" Regina stopped to examine her work.

"I don't know. Something about running in school," Todd replied. "How are you going to get this stupid bird to the science fair?"

"Carry it," Regina answered without hesitating. "It's big, but it's really light. I don't suppose you would help Beth and me?"

"I don't suppose I would," Todd told her, wrapping his hand around the broomstick that formed one bird leg.

"Hey—get your paws off!" Regina cried. "Leave it alone!"

Todd obediently backed away.

"You're just jealous because Christopher Robin is going to win the computer," Regina said.

"Listen, Reggie—you've *got* to tell me what Patrick MacKay is doing for his worm project," Todd pleaded. "You've *got* to."

She climbed down off the ladder. She saw the big worm in Todd's hand. "What's that for?" she demanded.

"Nothing." Todd's cheeks turned pink.

"You planned to drop that down my back, didn't you?" Regina accused him.

"No. I was just taking it for a walk," Todd told her. He laughed.

"You're a creep," Regina said, shaking her head. "Don't you ever get tired of those stupid worms?"

"No," Todd replied. "So tell me. What's Patrick's project?"

"You want to hear the truth?" Regina asked.

"Yeah."

"The truth is, I don't know," his sister confessed. "I really don't know *what* he's doing."

Todd stared hard at her for a long moment. "You really don't?"

She crossed her heart. "I really don't know."

Todd suddenly had an idea. "Where does he live?" he asked eagerly.

The question caught Regina by surprise. "Why?"

"Danny and I can go over there tonight," Todd said. "And I'll ask him what he's doing."

"You're going to go to his house?" Regina asked.

"I've *got* to find out!" Todd exclaimed. "I've worked so hard on my worm house, Reggie. I don't want Patrick the Copycat to do something better."

Regina eyed her brother thoughtfully. "And what will you do for *me* if I tell you where he lives?"

A grin spread over Todd's face. He held up the worm. "If you tell me, I won't put this down your back."

"Ha-ha," Regina replied, rolling her eyes. "You're a real pal, Todd."

"Tell me!" he insisted eagerly, grabbing her by the shoulders.

"Okay, okay. Don't have a cow. Patrick lives on Glen Cove," Regina replied. "I think the number is 100. It's a huge, old mansion. Behind a tall fence."

"Thanks!" Todd said. "Thanks a lot!"

Then, as Regina bent down to pick up the globs of papier-mâché from the garage floor, he dropped the worm down the back of her T-shirt.

"I can't believe we're doing this," Danny complained. "My parents said I couldn't come over. As soon as they went shopping, I ducked out. But if they catch me . . ." His voice trailed off.

"We'll be back home in fifteen minutes," Todd said. He changed gear and pedalled the bike harder. Danny's old bike splashed through a deep puddle at the kerb.

The rain clouds had rolled away. But the wind still gusted, cool and damp. The sun had set about an hour before. Now a thin sliver of moon hung low in the evening sky.

"Where is the house? On Glen Cove?" Danny asked, out of breath.

Todd nodded. He changed gear again. He liked changing back and forth. It was a new bike, and he still hadn't got used to so many gears.

A car rolled towards them rapidly, the glare of its white headlights forcing them to shield their eyes. Danny's bike rolled up on to the kerb, and he nearly toppled over. "Why'd they have their full beam on?" he griped.

"Beats me," Todd replied.

They turned sharply on to Glen Cove. It was a wide street of old houses set back on broad, sloping lawns. The houses were set far apart, separated by dark wooded areas.

"No streetlights," Danny commented. "You'd think rich people could afford streetlights."

"Maybe they like it dark," Todd replied thoughtfully. "You know. It helps keep people away."

"It's a bit creepy here," Danny said softly, leaning over his handlebars.

"Don't be a wimp. Look for 100," Todd said sharply. "That's Patrick's address."

"Wow. Check out that house!" Danny said, slowing down and pointing. "It looks like a castle!"

"I think 100 must be on the next block," Todd called, eagerly pedalling ahead.

"What are we going to say to Patrick?" Danny asked, breathing hard, struggling to catch up.

"I'm just going to ask him if we can see his worm project," Todd replied, his eyes searching the darkness for address signs. "Maybe I'll act like I want to help him out. You know. Give him a few tips on how to take care of the worms."

"Nice of you," Danny teased. He chuckled to himself. "What if Patrick says no?"

Todd didn't reply. He hadn't thought of that.

He squeezed the hand brake. "Look." He pointed to an enormous house behind a tall iron fence. "That's his house."

Danny's brakes squealed as he brought his bike to a stop. He lowered his feet to the wet pavement. "Wow."

The house rose up over the broad, tree-filled lawn, black against the purple night sky. It was completely dark. Not a light on anywhere.

"No one at home," Danny said, whispering.

"Good," Todd replied. "This is even better. Maybe we can look down through the basement window or find the window to Patrick's room, and see what he's working on."

"Maybe," Danny replied reluctantly.

Todd glanced around. Patrick's house was the only one on the block. And it was surrounded by woods.

Both boys climbed off their bikes and started to walk them to the driveway.

"I can't believe Patrick would live in such a wreck of a place," Todd said, pulling off his cap and scratching his hair. "I mean, this house is a real dump."

"Maybe his parents are weird or something," Danny suggested as they parked their bikes.

"Maybe," Todd replied thoughtfully.

"Sometimes rich people get a little weird," Danny said, climbing on to the porch and ringing the doorbell.

"How would *you* know?" Todd said, sniggering. He pulled his cap back down over his dark hair and rang the bell again. "No answer. Let's check out the back," he said, hopping off the porch.

"What for?" Danny demanded.

"Let's just look in the windows," Todd urged, moving along to the side of the house. "Let's see if we can see anything at all."

As they turned the corner, it grew even darker. The pale sliver of moonlight was reflected in one of the upstairs windows. The only light.

"This is stupid," Danny complained. "It's too dark to see anything inside the house. And, besides—"

He stopped.

"*Now* what's wrong?" Todd demanded impatiently.

"Didn't you hear it? I heard it again," Danny said. "Like a growl. Some kind of animal growl."

Todd didn't hear the growl.

But he saw something enormous running towards them.

He saw the evil red glow of its eyes—unblinking eyes trained on him.

And he knew it was too late to escape.

"Run!" Danny screamed.

But Todd couldn't move.

As the enormous red-eyed monster bounded towards them, Todd pressed his back against a side door.

He nearly fell as the door swung in.

The creature uttered an ugly, threatening growl. Its huge paws thundered over the ground.

"Inside!" Todd screamed. "Danny—get in the house!"

His heart pounding as loudly as the monster's paws, Todd scrambled into the dark house. Danny lurched in behind him, uttering low gasps.

Todd slammed the door shut as the creature attacked.

Its paws struck the windowpane in the door, making the entire door rattle.

"It's a dog!" Todd cried in a choked whisper. "A huge, angry dog!"

31

The dog let out another ferocious growl and leaped at the door. Its paws scraped over the window.

"A dog?" Danny exclaimed shrilly. "I thought it was a *gorilla!*"

The two boys pressed their shoulders against the door, holding it shut. They peered out warily at the big creature.

The dog had sat back on its haunches. It stared in at them, its red eyes glowing. It was panting loudly, its enormous tongue hanging out of its mouth.

"Someone should put that dog on a diet!" Danny exclaimed.

"We could ride him to school!" Todd added.

"How do we get out of here?" Danny asked, turning away from the dog. His eyes searched the dark room.

"He'll go away," Todd said. He swallowed hard. "Probably."

"This place is a dump," Danny said, stepping into the room.

Todd turned to follow Danny. They were in the kitchen, he saw. Pale moonlight floated in through the window. Even in this dim light, Todd could see that something was terribly wrong.

The kitchen counters were bare and covered in dust. There were no appliances—no toaster, no microwave, no refrigerator. There were no dishes or pots and pans in view. Glancing down, Todd saw that the sink was caked with thick dirt.

"Weird," Danny muttered.

The two boys made their way through a short hallway to the dining room.

"Where's the furniture?" Danny asked, gazing in all directions.

The room was empty.

"Maybe they're redecorating or something," Todd guessed.

"This doesn't make sense. Patrick's family is rich," Danny said, shaking his head. "You know how neat Patrick is. He gets upset if his shirt comes untucked."

"I don't get it," Todd replied. "Where do you think he has his worm project?"

The two boys made their way towards the living room. Their trainers scraped over the dusty, bare floor.

"Something is weird here," Danny murmured. "Something is very weird."

They both gasped as they stepped into the living room—and saw the figure hunched at the window.

Saw the decayed green flesh of his face.

Saw the bones of his jaw, open in a hideous toothless grin.

Saw his evil, sunken eyes staring across the room at them.

33

The heavy silence was broken by the shrill screams of the two boys.

"Go! Go!" Todd cried. He shoved Danny towards the door and stumbled along behind him, keeping his hands on Danny's shoulders.

"Go! Go! Go!"

Through the bare dining room. Across the dust-covered kitchen.

"Go! Go!"

Todd grabbed the doorknob, pulled open the door, and they both burst out of the house.

Had the dog left?

Yes!

"Let's *move*!" Todd cried.

But Danny needed no encouragement. He was already halfway down the driveway, his chubby legs pumping hard, his hands stretched out in front of him as if trying to *pull* himself to safety.

Out of the gate. On to their bikes.

They pedalled furiously. Faster. Faster. Until

their legs ached and they could barely breathe.

And they never looked back.

Who was that hideous, decayed figure in Patrick's house?

And why was the house so dusty, so totally bare?

Todd spent most of the night lying awake in his bed, thinking about it.

But the mystery wasn't cleared up until the next morning.

Yawning sleepily, Todd pulled on the same clothes he had worn the day before. Then he made his way down the hall to go to breakfast.

He stopped outside Regina's bedroom door when he heard her laughing. At first, he thought she was talking to herself.

But then he realized that Regina was on the phone.

So early?

He pressed his ear to the door and listened.

"Isn't it a riot, Beth?" Regina was saying. "I sent them to the wrong address." Regina laughed again. Gleeful laughter.

Todd suddenly snapped wide awake. He pressed his ear tighter against the bedroom door.

"Todd was so desperate, I couldn't resist," Regina was saying. "Know where I sent them?"

There was a short pause. Todd realized he was

35

holding his breath. He let it out silently and took another one, listening hard.

"I sent them to the old Fosgate mansion," Regina told Beth. She laughed. "Yeah. Right. That old deserted mansion where those kids had that Halloween party. Yeah. You know. They left that dummy with the weird mask in the window."

Another pause.

Todd gritted his teeth as he listened to his sister's triumphant laughter. He could feel every muscle in his body tightening in anger.

"I don't know, Beth. I haven't talked to him yet," Regina was saying. "I heard Todd come in last night. He ran straight to his room and shut the door. He was probably too scared to talk!"

More laughter.

Clenching and unclenching his fists, Todd stepped away from his sister's door. He stopped at the stairs, feeling his face grow red-hot. He was thinking hard.

So Reggie played a little joke on Danny and me, he thought bitterly. So she gave me the wrong address and sent us to that old haunted house.

Ha-ha. Good joke.

Todd felt so angry, he wanted to scream.

Now Regina will be laughing at me about this for ever, he realized. She will make fun of me for the rest of my life.

Her bedroom door opened, and Regina stepped out into the hall. She was pulling her brown hair back into a ponytail.

She stopped when she saw Todd at the top of the stairs. "So, how did it go last night?" she asked him, grinning.

"Fine," he replied casually. He gave her an innocent, wide-eyed stare.

Her grin faded. "Did you go to Patrick's house? Did you talk to him about his worm project?" she demanded, staring back at him, studying his face.

Todd shook his head. "No. Danny and I decided to skip it. We just stayed at Danny's," he lied.

Her dark eyes seemed to dim. She bit her lower lip. Todd could see how disappointed she was.

He turned and made his way down the stairs, feeling a little better.

You want to play jokes, Reggie? he thought. Okay. Fine.

But now it's *my* turn. My turn to play a mean joke.

Todd smiled. He had already thought of a really good one.

Todd hoisted the cardboard box in both hands.
His worm house was packed carefully inside. It
was heavier than he thought.

"Where shall I put it?" he asked Mrs Sanger,
struggling to keep the heavy box from slipping
out of his hands.

"What? I can't hear you!" The science teacher
held a clipboard in one hand. She cupped her
other hand around her mouth as a megaphone.

It was deafening in the gym as the kids all
hurried to set up their science projects in time for
the expo. Excited voices competed with scraping
chairs and tables, the rattle of boxes being
unpacked, and projects of all shapes and sizes
being assembled and set up.

"What a crowd!" Todd exclaimed.

"I can't hear you!" Mrs Sanger shouted. She
pointed to a long table against the wall. "I think
your project goes there, Todd."

Todd started to say something. But he was

interrupted by the crash of shattering glass and a girl's loud scream.

"Was that the *acid*?" Mrs Sanger shouted, her eyes going wide with horror. "Was that the acid?" She pushed past Todd and went tearing across the gym, holding her clipboard in front of her like a shield.

Todd watched a lot of kids gathering around the spot of the accident. Mrs Sanger burst into the circle, and everyone began talking at once.

Around the vast gym, others ignored the excitement and continued feverishly setting up their projects.

The benches had been put out. Some parents and other kids from the school were already seated, waiting to watch the expo and the judging of projects.

Groaning, Todd started to make his way through the crowded gym carrying the cardboard box. He had to stop and chuckle when he caught a glimpse of Regina and Beth.

They had their enormous robin set up close to the benches. The head was the right size now. They had managed to shave it down smoothly.

But some of the tail feathers had got mashed. And they were working frantically to smooth them out.

What losers, Todd thought, grinning.

There's no way they're going to win the computer.

Turning away, he glimpsed Danny's balloon solar system hanging on the back wall. One of the balloons—the one closest to the sun—had already deflated.

Pitiful, Todd thought, shaking his head. That's just pitiful.

He sighed. Poor Danny. I guess I should have let him share my project.

Todd lowered the box on to the table reserved for him.

"Ten minutes, everyone! Ten minutes!" Mrs Sanger was shouting.

No problem, Todd thought.

He opened the box and carefully lifted out the worm house. What a beauty! he thought proudly.

It looked like a perfect little house. Todd had polished the wood frame until it glowed. And he had cleaned the glass until it was spotless.

He put the worm house down carefully on the table and turned it so that the glass side faced the audience on the benches. He gazed into it. He could see the long brown and purple worms crawling from room to room.

He had packed the dirt in carefully. Then he had dropped in more than twenty worms before sealing it all up.

It's a real big family! he thought, grinning.

Once the worm house was in place, Todd pulled out the sign he had made for it and placed the sign beside it on the table.

He stepped back to admire his work. But someone pushed him gently aside.

"Make room. Make room, Todd." It was Mrs Sanger. And to Todd's surprise, she was helping Patrick MacKay carry a long cardboard box to the table.

"Move your project to the side, Todd," the teacher instructed. "You have to share the table."

"Huh? Share?" Todd hesitated.

"Hurry—please!" Mrs Sanger pleaded. "Patrick's box is heavy."

"I'm sharing the table with Patrick?" Todd couldn't hide his unhappiness.

Obediently, he slid his worm house to one side of the table. Then he stood behind the table, watching as Patrick and the teacher unloaded the long box. It was nearly two metres long.

"Is that all *one* worm?" Todd joked.

"Very funny," Patrick muttered. He was straining hard to lift his project on to the table.

"This will be our worm table," Mrs Sanger said, grabbing the end of the box and tugging. Patrick pulled, too.

Todd gasped as Patrick hoisted his project on to the tabletop.

"Very impressive, Patrick," Mrs Sanger commented, straightening her skirt. She hurried off to help someone else.

Todd gaped at the project. It towered over his. It was nearly two metres tall, taller than Patrick!

"Oh, nooooo," Todd moaned to himself. He turned to Patrick. "It—it isn't . . . it *can't* be—!" He choked on the words.

Patrick was busily setting up his sign. He stepped back, checking it out, making sure it was straight.

"Yes, it is!" he said, beaming at Todd. "It's a worm skyscraper!"

"Wow." Todd didn't want to show how upset he was. But he couldn't help it. His legs were trembling. His mouth dropped open. And he started to stutter. "But—but—but—"

I don't believe this! Todd thought miserably.

I built a crummy little worm house. And Patrick made a skyscraper!

It's not fair! *Not fair!*

Patrick doesn't even *like* worms!

He stared at the giant wood-and-glass structure. He could see dozens and dozens of worms inside. They were crawling from floor to floor. There was even a wooden lift with several worms tucked inside.

"Todd—are you okay?" Patrick asked.

"Yeah. Uh . . . fine," Todd replied, trying to force his legs to stop quivering.

"You look a little weird," Patrick said, staring at Todd with his bright blue eyes.

"Uh . . . that's a nice project, Patrick," Todd admitted through clenched teeth. "You could win the big prize."

"You think so?" Patrick replied, as if the thought had never occurred to him. "Thanks, Todd. I got the idea from you. About worms, I mean."

You *stole* the idea, you thief! Todd thought angrily.

I have only one wish for you, Patrick. *Go eat worms!*

"Wow! What's *that*?" Danny's voice broke into Todd's ugly thoughts. He was staring in amazement at Patrick's project.

"It's a worm skyscraper," Patrick told him, beaming with pride.

Danny admired it for a while. Then he turned to Todd. "Why didn't *you* think of that?" he whispered.

Todd gave Danny a hard shove. "Go blow up a balloon," he muttered.

Danny spun around angrily. "Don't shove me—"

Mrs Sanger's voice over the loudspeaker rose over the noise of the gym. "Places by your projects, everyone. The expo is starting. The judges will begin their rounds."

Danny hurried back to his balloon solar system against the wall. Todd watched him make his way past a display of rocks. Danny

43

was swinging his arms as he walked, and he nearly knocked over all the rocks.

Then Todd stepped behind the table. He brushed a speck of dust off the roof of his worm house.

I should just toss it in the trash, he thought miserably. He glanced at Patrick, who stood beside him, grinning from ear to ear, his hands resting on the sides of his magnificent skyscraper.

The copycat is going to win, Todd thought sadly.

He sighed. Only one thing would cheer him up a little. One thing. And gazing across the gym, Todd saw that it was time for it to happen.

The three judges—all teachers from another school—were stepping up to check out Christopher Robin. As they bent low to examine the papier-mâché bird's feet, Todd made his way quickly over to his sister's project.

He wanted a good view.

One judge, a plump young woman in a bright yellow top, examined the tail feathers. Another judge, a man with a shiny bald head, was questioning Regina and Beth. The third judge had her back to Todd. She was running her hand over the bird's swelling orange breast.

Reggie and Beth look really nervous, Todd thought, edging past a display on how trash gets recycled.

Well, they *should* be nervous. What a stupid project.

Todd stopped a few metres in front of the benches. There was a really big audience for the expo, he noticed. The benches were at least two-thirds filled. Mostly parents and younger brothers and sisters of the contestants.

The bald judge kept making notes on a small pad as he questioned Regina and Beth. The other two judges were staring up at the giant robin's beak.

Todd edged closer.

"What's this string?" the judge in the yellow top asked Beth.

"Huh? String?" Beth reacted with surprise. She and Regina raised their eyes to the yellow beak.

"What string?" Regina demanded.

Too late.

The judge in the yellow top pulled the string.

The beak lowered, revealing a surprise inside.

"Ohhhh."

"Yuck!"

Disgusted groans rose up from the audience. And Regina and Beth started to scream.

45

Fat worms wriggled out from inside the bird's beak.

Some of them wriggled out and rained down on the judges.

A huge purple worm plopped on to the bald judge's head. The angry judge's red face darkened until it nearly matched the purple worm.

Early that morning, Todd had packed about thirty worms in there. He was glad to see that most of them had stayed in the beak.

People on the benches were groaning and moaning. "That's *sick!*" someone yelled.

"Disgusting! That's so disgusting!" a little boy kept repeating.

The judges were demanding to know if Regina and Beth had stuffed the worms up there as a joke.

Mrs Sanger was glaring angrily at them. The two girls were sputtering their apologies.

It was a thrilling moment, Todd thought. A thrilling moment.

About ten or fifteen worms were wriggling across the gym floor. Todd started to edge back to his table.

"There he is! My brother!" he heard Regina shout. He glanced up to see her pointing furiously at him. "Todd did it! It had to be Todd!"

He gave her an innocent shrug. "I thought Christopher Robin looked hungry—so I fed him!" he called. Then he hurried back to his worm house.

A big grin on his handsome face, Patrick slapped Todd a high five. "Good stuff!"

Todd grudgingly accepted the congratulations. He didn't want to be friends with Patrick. He wanted Patrick to go eat worms.

He glanced back at Danny. Danny was frantically blowing up a balloon. The rings had fallen off Saturn. And someone had accidentally popped Pluto.

Todd smiled. He felt pretty good. His little joke had worked perfectly. Revenge was sweet. He had paid Regina back for sending him to that creepy old house.

But his smile faded as he glanced at Patrick's skyscraper and remembered that he was going to miss out on the grand prize.

It took the school janitor a few minutes to

round up all the worms. The crowd on the benches cheered him on as he scooped up the wiggling worms one by one and dropped them into an empty coffee jar.

After that, the expo continued calmly and quietly. The judges moved from project to project, asking questions, making notes.

Todd took a deep breath when they approached his table. Don't get excited, he warned himself. The worm house looks really puny next to the worm skyscraper.

He had a sudden urge to bump the table, to shake it really hard. Maybe the skyscraper would topple over, and the house would be left standing.

I could pretend it was just an accident, Todd thought.

Evil thoughts.

But he didn't do it.

The three judges spent about ten seconds looking at Todd's project. They didn't ask Todd a single question.

Then they gazed at Patrick's skyscraper for at least five minutes. "How did you get all those worms in there?" the bald judge asked.

"I love the elevator!"

"How many worms are there in total?"

"Can worms survive in a *real* skyscraper?"

"And what does this project prove about gravity?"

Yak yak yak, Todd thought bitterly.

He watched the judges coo and carry on over Patrick's project. He wanted to grab all three of them and say, "He's a copycat! I'm the real worm guy! I'm the one who likes worms!"

But he just stood there grinding his teeth, tapping his fingers tensely on the tabletop.

Still scribbling notes about Patrick's project, the judges moved on to the next project—Liquids and Gases.

Patrick turned to Todd and forced him into slapping another high five. "You can come over and see my new computer any time," Patrick whispered confidently.

Todd forced a weak laugh. He turned away from Patrick—and found his sister glaring at him furiously from the other side of the table.

"How *could* you, Todd!" she demanded, spitting out the words, her hands pressed tightly at her waist. "How could you do that to Beth and me?"

"Easy," he replied, unable to keep a grin off his face.

"You *ruined* our project!" Regina cried.

"I know," Todd said, still grinning. "You deserved it."

Regina started to sputter.

The loudspeaker above their heads crackled on. "Ladies and gentlemen, we have a winner!" Mrs Sanger declared.

The huge gym grew silent. No one moved.

"The judges have a winner!" Mrs Sanger repeated, her voice booming off the tile walls. "The grand-prize winner of this year's Science Expo is . . ."

12

"The winner is . . ." Mrs Sanger announced, "Danny Fletcher and his Balloon Solar System!"

The audience on the benches was quiet for a moment, but then erupted in cheers and applause. Todd's classmates on the floor applauded, too.

Todd turned and caught the startled expression on Danny's face. Several kids rushed forward to congratulate Danny. The balloons bobbed behind Danny as he grinned and took a funny bow.

The gym erupted as everyone began to talk at once. Then the spectators made their way down from the benches and began wandering through the displays.

I don't *believe* this! Todd thought. Glancing at Patrick, he saw that Patrick felt the same way.

Danny flashed Todd a thumbs-up sign. Todd returned it, shaking his head.

He felt a hard shove on his shoulders.

"Hey—" he cried out angrily and spun round. "Are you still here?"

Regina glared at him angrily. "That's for ruining our project!" she shouted.

She shoved him again. "You apologize!" she demanded furiously.

He laughed. "No way!"

She growled at him and raised her fists. "Go eat worms!" she screamed.

Still laughing, he pulled off the wooden back of his worm house and lifted up a long, brown worm. He dangled it in front of his sister's face. "Here. Have some dessert."

With a furious cry, Regina completely lost all control.

She leaped at Todd, shoving him over backwards.

He cried out as he sprawled back—and hit the table hard.

Several kids let out startled screams as the enormous worm skyscraper tilted . . . tilted . . . tilted . . .

"No!" Patrick screamed. He reached out both hands to stop it.

And missed.

And the heavy wood-and-glass structure toppled on to the next table with a deafening crash of shattered glass.

"No!" a girl screamed. "That's Liquids and

Gases! Look out—it's Liquids and Gases!"

Dirt poured out of the broken skyscraper. Several worms came wriggling out on to the table.

As Todd pulled himself to his feet, wild screams filled the gym.

"Liquids and Gases!"

"What's that smoke?"

"What did they break? Did they break a window?"

"Liquids and Gases!"

Thick, white smoke poured up from a broken glass bottle under the fallen skyscraper.

"Everybody out!" someone yelled. "Everybody out! It's going to blow up!"

13

No one was hurt in the explosion.

Some strange gases escaped, and it smelled pretty weird in the gym for a while.

A lot of worms went flying across the room. And there was a lot of broken glass to be cleaned up.

But it was a minor explosion, Todd told his parents later. "Really. No big deal," he said. "I'm sure everyone will forget all about it in five or ten years."

A few days later, carrying a small, white box in both hands, Todd made his way down the basement stairs. He could hear the steady *plonk plonk* of ping-pong balls against bats.

Regina and Beth glanced up from their game as he entered the room. "Chinese food?" Beth asked, spotting the little box.

"No. Worms," Todd replied, crossing the room to his worm tank.

"Are you still into worms?" Beth demanded, twirling her ping-pong bat. "Even after what happened at the Science Expo?"

"It all got cleaned up," Todd snapped. "It was no big deal."

"Hah!" Regina cried scornfully.

Todd gazed at his sister in surprise. "Hey, are you talking to me again?" Regina was so furious, she hadn't said a word to him since the big disaster.

"No. I am not talking to you," Regina replied with a sneer. "I will never talk to you again."

"Give me a break!" Todd muttered. He opened the box and poured the new worms into the big glass aquarium where he stored his collection.

Plonk. Plonk. The girls returned to their game.

"You know, what happened at the Science Expo was no tragedy," Todd called to them. "Some people thought it was pretty funny." He sniggered.

"Some people are pretty *sick*," Beth muttered.

Regina slammed the ball hard. It sailed into the net. "You ruined everything," she accused Todd angrily. "You ruined the whole expo."

"And you ruined our project," Beth added, reaching for the ball. "You made us look like total jerks."

55

"So?" Todd replied, laughing.

The girls didn't laugh.

"I only did it because you sent Danny and me to that creepy old house," Todd told them. He used a small trowel to soften the dirt in the worm tank.

"Well, you wouldn't have won, anyway," Regina said, sneering. "Patrick's skyscraper made your puny house look like a baby's project."

"You're jealous of Patrick—aren't you, Todd?" Beth accused him.

"Jealous of that copycat?" Todd cried. "He doesn't know one end of a worm from another!"

The girls started their game again. Beth took a wild swing and sent the ball sailing across the room.

Todd caught it with his free hand. "Come here," he said. "I'll show you something cool."

"No way," Regina replied nastily.

"Just toss back the ball," Beth said, holding up her hand to catch it.

"Come here. This is really cool," Todd insisted, grinning.

He pulled a long worm out of the tank and held it up in the air. It wriggled and squirmed, trying to get free.

Regina and Beth didn't move away from the table. But he saw that they were watching him.

Todd set the long worm down on the table and picked up a pocket knife. "You watching?" With one quick motion, he sliced the worm in half.

"Yuck!" Beth cried, making a disgusted face.

"You're sick!" Regina declared. "You're really sick, Todd."

"Watch!" Todd instructed.

All three of them stared at the tabletop as the two worm halves wriggled off in different directions.

"See?" Todd cried, laughing. "Now there are *two* of them!"

"Sick. Really sick," his sister muttered.

"That's disgusting, Todd," Beth agreed, shaking her head.

"But wouldn't it be cool if people could do that?" Todd exclaimed. "You know. Your bottom half goes to school, and your top half stays at home and watches TV!"

"Hey! Look at that!" Regina cried suddenly. She pointed to the glass worm tank.

"Huh? What?" Todd demanded, lowering his eyes to the worms.

"Those worms—they were watching you!" Regina exclaimed. "See? They're sort of staring at you."

"Don't be stupid," Todd muttered. But he saw that Regina was right. Three of the worms had their heads raised out of the dirt and seemed to be staring up at him. "You have a weird imagination," Todd insisted.

"No. They were watching," Regina insisted excitedly. "I saw them watching you when you cut that worm in two."

"Worms can't see!" Todd told them. "They weren't watching me. That's stupid! That's—"

"But they *were*!" Regina cried.

"The worms are angry," Beth added, glancing at Regina. "The worms don't like to see their friend cut in half."

"Stop," Todd pleaded. "Just give me a break, okay?"

"The worms are going to get revenge, Todd," Regina said. "They saw what you did. Now they're planning their revenge."

Todd let out a scornful laugh. "You must think I'm as stupid as you are!" he declared. "There's no way I'm going to fall for that. No way I'm going to believe such a stupid idea."

Giggling to each other, Regina and Beth returned to their ping-pong game.

Todd dropped the two worm halves into the tank. To his surprise, four more worms had poked up out of the soft dirt. They were staring straight up at him.

Todd stared down at them, thinking about what Regina and Beth had said.

What a stupid idea, he thought. Those worms weren't watching me.

Or *were* they?

"Todd—rise and shine!"

Todd blinked his eyes open. He sat up slowly in bed and stretched his arms over his head.

"Rise and shine, Todd! Look alive!" his mother called from the foot of the stairs.

Why does she say the same thing every morning? he wondered. Always "Rise and shine, rise and shine!" Why can't she say, "Time to get up!" or, "Move 'em on out!" or something? Just for a little variety.

Grumpily, he pulled himself up and lowered his feet to the floor.

Why can't I have a clock radio like Regina? he asked himself. Then I could wake up to music instead of "Rise and shine!"

"Look alive up there!" Mrs Barstow called impatiently.

"I'm up! I'm up, Mum!" Todd shouted hoarsely down to her.

Bright sunlight poured in through the bedroom window. Squinting towards the window, he could see a patch of clear blue sky.

Nice day, he thought.

What day is it? he asked himself, standing up and stretching some more. Thursday? Yeah. Thursday.

Good, he thought. We have gym on Thursday. Maybe we'll play softball.

Gym was Todd's favourite class—especially on days they went outside.

His pyjama bottoms had become totally twisted. He straightened them as he made his way to the bathroom to brush his teeth.

Are we having the maths test today or tomorrow? he wondered, squinting at his sleepy face in the medicine cabinet mirror. I hope it's tomorrow. I forgot to study for it last night.

He stuck his tongue out at himself.

He could hear Regina downstairs, arguing about something with their mother. Regina liked to argue in the morning. It was the way she got her mind into gear.

She argued about what to wear. Or what she wanted for breakfast. One of her favourite arguments was whether or not it was too warm to wear a jacket.

Todd's mother never learned. She always argued back. So they had pretty noisy mornings.

Todd liked to sleep as long as possible. Then he

took his time getting dressed. That way, Regina had usually finished all her arguing by the time he came downstairs.

Thinking about the maths test, he brushed his teeth. Then he returned to his room and pulled on a clean pair of faded jeans and a navy blue T-shirt that came down nearly to his knees.

Regina and Mrs Barstow were still arguing as Todd entered the kitchen. Regina, her dark hair tied back in a single plait, sat at the table, finishing her breakfast. Their mother, dressed for work, stood on the other side of the table, a steaming cup of coffee in one hand.

"But I'm too hot in that jacket!" Regina was insisting.

"Then why not wear a sweatshirt?" their mother suggested patiently.

"I don't have any," Regina complained.

"You have a whole drawerful!" Mrs Barstow protested.

"But I don't like those!" Regina cried shrilly.

Todd grabbed his glass of orange juice off the table and gulped it down in one long swallow.

"Todd, sit down and have your breakfast," his mother ordered.

"Can't. I'm late," he said, wiping orange juice off his upper lip with one hand. "Got to go."

"But you haven't brushed your hair!" Mrs Barstow exclaimed.

Regina, chewing on a piece of rye toast, laughed. "How can you tell?"

Todd ignored her. "No need," he told his mother. "I'm wearing my Raiders cap." He glanced towards the hook on the hallway wall where he thought he had left it. Not there.

"I can't believe the school lets you wear your cap all day," Mrs Barstow murmured, refilling her coffee cup.

"They don't care," Todd told her.

"Only the real grunges wear caps," Regina reported.

"Is your brother a grunge?" their mother asked, raising her eyes over the white mug as she sipped coffee.

"Has anyone seen my Raiders cap?" Todd asked quickly, before Regina could answer.

"Isn't it on the hook?" Mrs Barstow asked, glancing towards the hall.

Todd shook his head. "Maybe I left it upstairs." He turned and hurried towards the front stairs.

"Come back and eat your cereal! It's getting soggy!" his mother called.

Grabbing on to the banister, Todd took the stairs two at a time. Standing in the doorway to his room, his eyes searched the bed. The top of the chest of drawers.

No cap.

He was halfway to the wardrobe when he

spotted it on the floor. I must have tossed it there before going to bed, he remembered.

Bending down, he picked up the cap and slid it down over his hair.

He knew at once that something was wrong.

Something felt funny.

As he bent the peak down the way he liked it, he felt something move in his hair.

Something wet.

It felt as if his hair had come to life and had started to crawl around under the cap.

Moving quickly to the mirror over the chest of drawers, Todd pulled the cap away—and stared in shock at the fat, brown worms wriggling through his hair.

Todd shook his head hard. A shudder of surprise.

One of the worms toppled from his hair and slid down his forehead, dropping on to the chest of drawers.

"I don't believe this," Todd muttered out loud.

He tossed the cap to the floor. Then he reached up with both hands and carefully began untangling the worms from his hair.

"Regina!" he screamed. "Regina—you're going to pay for this!"

He pulled three worms off his head, then picked up the fourth from the chest of drawers. "Yuck." He made a disgusted face into the mirror. His hair was damp and sticky where the worms had crawled.

"Okay, Reggie! I'm coming!" he shouted as he bounded down the stairs, the worms dangling in one fist.

She glanced up casually from the table as Todd burst into the kitchen.

"Your cereal is really getting soggy," his mother said from the sink. "You'd better—" She stopped when she saw the worms in Todd's hand.

"Very funny, Regina!" Todd exclaimed angrily. He shoved the fistful of worms under his sister's nose.

"Yuck! Get away!" she shrieked.

"Todd—get those worms away from the table!" Mrs Barstow demanded sharply. "What's *wrong* with you? You know better than that!"

"Don't yell at *me*!" Todd screeched at his mother. "Yell at *her*!" He pointed furiously at his sister.

"Me?" Regina's eyes opened wide in innocence. "What did I do?"

Todd let out an angry groan and turned to face his mother. "She stuffed worms in my cap!" he exclaimed, shaking the worms in Mrs Barstow's face.

"Huh?" Regina cried furiously. "That's a *lie*!"

Todd and Regina began screaming accusations at each other.

Mrs Barstow stepped between them. "Quiet—please!" she demanded. "Please!"

"But—but—!" Todd sputtered.

"Todd, you're going to squeeze those poor

66

worms to death!" Mrs Barstow declared. "Go and put them away in the basement. Then take a deep breath, count to ten, and come back."

Todd grumbled under his breath. But he obediently headed down to the basement.

When he returned to the kitchen a minute later, Regina was still denying that she had loaded the cap with worms. She turned to Todd, a solemn expression on her face. "I swear, Todd," she said, "it wasn't me."

"Yeah. Sure," Todd muttered. "Then who else did it? Dad? Do you think Dad filled my cap with worms before he went to work?"

The idea was so ridiculous, it made all three of them laugh.

Mrs Barstow put her hands on Todd's shoulders and guided him into his seat at the table. "Cereal," she said softly. "Eat your cereal. You're going to be late."

"Leave my worms alone," Todd told his sister in a low voice. He pulled the chair in and picked up the spoon. "I mean it, Reggie. I hate your stupid jokes. And I don't like people messing with my worms."

Regina sighed wearily. "I don't mess with your disgusting worms," she shot back. "I told you—I didn't do it."

"Let's just drop it, okay?" Mrs Barstow pleaded. "Look at the clock."

"But why should she get away with that,

Mum?" Todd demanded. "Why should she be allowed to—"

"Because I didn't do it!" Regina interrupted.

"You *must* have done it!" Todd screamed.

"I think you did it yourself," Regina suggested with a sneer. "I think you stuffed worms in your own cap."

"Oh, that's good! That's good!" Todd cried sarcastically. "Why, Regina? Why would I do that?"

"To get me in trouble," Regina replied.

Todd gaped at her, speechless.

"You're *both* going to be in trouble if you don't drop this discussion—right now," their mother insisted.

"Okay. We'll drop it," Todd grumbled, glaring at his sister.

He dipped the spoon into the cereal. "Totally soggy," he muttered. "How I am supposed to—"

Regina's shrill scream cut off Todd's complaint.

He followed her horrified gaze down to his bowl—where he found a fat purple worm floating on top of the milk.

Todd tried to concentrate at school, but he kept thinking about the worms.

Of *course* it had to be Regina who had put the worms in his cap and in his cereal bowl.

But she had acted so shocked. And she said again and again that she didn't know anything about them.

Todd kept thinking about the afternoon in the basement. About cutting the worm in half. About the other worms watching him from their glass tank.

"They saw what you did," his sister had said in a low, frightened voice. "And now they're planning their revenge."

That's so stupid, Todd thought, pretending to read his social studies text.

So stupid.

But thinking about Regina's words gave him a chill.

And thinking about the worms waiting in his

cap, crawling so wetly through his hair, made Todd feel a little sick.

He told Danny all about it at lunch.

They sat across from each other in the noisy lunchroom. Danny unpacked his lunch from the brown paper lunch bag and examined the sandwich. "Ham and cheese again," he groaned. "Every day Mum gives me ham and cheese."

"Why don't you ask for something else?" Todd suggested.

"I don't like anything else," Danny replied, tearing open his bag of crisps.

Todd unpacked his lunch, too. But he left it untouched as he told Danny about the worms.

Danny laughed at first. "Your sister is such a pain," he said through a mouthful of crisps.

"I suppose you're right," Todd replied thoughtfully. "It's *got* to be Regina. But she acted so surprised. I mean, she *screamed* when she saw the worm floating in the cereal."

"She probably practised screaming all day yesterday," Danny said, chomping into his sandwich.

Todd unwrapped the tinfoil from his sandwich. Peanut butter and jam. "Yeah. Maybe," he said, frowning.

"Come on, Todd," Danny said, mustard dripping down his chin. "That worm tank of yours is really deep. The worms didn't crawl out all by themselves. And they didn't crawl upstairs to your room and then find your hat and crawl inside."

"You're right. You're right," Todd said, still frowning thoughtfully. He pushed back his Raiders cap and scratched his brown hair. "But I just keep seeing those worms staring at me, and—"

"Worms don't have eyes!" Danny declared. "And they don't have faces. And, mainly, they don't have brains!"

Todd laughed. Danny was completely right, he realized.

The idea of worms planning to get their revenge was just ridiculous.

Feeling a lot better, he slid down in the chair and started his lunch. "Let's talk about something else," he said, taking a long drink from his carton of juice. He raised his peanut butter and jam sandwich to his mouth and took a big bite.

"Did you see Dawkins fall off his chair this morning?" Danny asked, sniggering.

Todd grinned. "Yeah. Miss Grant jumped so high, her head nearly hit the ceiling! I thought she was going to drop her teeth!"

"Luckily Dawkins landed on his head!" Danny exclaimed, wiping the mustard off his chin with the back of one hand. "Dawkins can't stay on a chair. No balance, or something. Every day he—"

Danny stopped when he saw the sick expression on Todd's face. "Hey, Todd—what's the matter?"

"Th-this peanut butter sandwich," Todd stammered. "It . . . tastes kind of strange."

"Huh?" Danny lowered his eyes to the half-eaten sandwich in Todd's hand.

Reluctantly, Todd pulled apart the two slices of bread.

Both boys moaned in disgust and let out hoarse gagging sounds as they saw the half-eaten purple worm curled up in the peanut butter.

"Have you seen my sister?" Todd asked a group of kids at the door that led out to the playground.

They all shook their heads no.

After angrily tossing away his lunch, Todd had run out of the lunchroom in search of Regina. He had to let her know that her stupid joke had gone too far.

Putting a worm in his peanut butter wasn't the least bit funny. It was *sick*.

As he ran through the halls, searching in each room for her, Todd could still taste the faintly sour flavour of the worm, could still feel its soft squishy body between his teeth.

It made his teeth itch. It made him feel itchy all over.

Regina, you're not getting away with this! he thought bitterly.

By the time he reached the end of the hallway, he felt so angry, he was seeing red.

He pushed past the group of kids, opened the

door, and burst outside. The bright afternoon sunlight made him lower his cap to shield his eyes.

He searched the playground for his sister.

Some kids from his class were playing a loud, frantic kickball game on the softball diamond. Jerry Dawkins and a few other guys called to Todd to join the game.

But he waved them off and kept running. He was in no mood for games.

Regina—where are you?

He circled the entire playground and teacher car park before he gave up. Then he slowly, unhappily, trudged back towards the school building.

His stomach growled and churned.

He could picture the worm half wriggling around inside him.

All around, kids were yelling and laughing and having fun.

They didn't eat worms for lunch, Todd thought bitterly. They don't have a mean, vicious sister who tries to ruin their lives.

He was nearly to the door, walking slowly, his head bowed, when he spotted Regina standing in the shade at the corner of the building.

He stopped and watched her. She was talking to someone. Then she started to laugh.

Keeping against the redbrick wall, Todd edged

a little closer. He could see two others in the shade with Regina.

Beth and Patrick.

All three of them were laughing now.

What was so funny?

Todd could feel the rage boiling up in him. As he crept closer, trying to hear what they were saying, he clenched his hands into tight, angry fists.

Pressing against the building, Todd stopped and listened.

Regina said something. He couldn't make out the words.

He took a step closer. Then one more.

And he heard Beth laugh and say, "So Todd doesn't know you're doing it?"

And then Patrick replied, "No. Todd doesn't know. He doesn't know I'm doing it."

Stunned, Todd jammed his back against the brick wall.

Patrick?

How can *Patrick* be doing it? Todd wondered. That's impossible! Unless . . .

Todd couldn't hold back any longer. He angrily stepped forward, feeling his face grow red-hot.

The three of them turned in surprise.

"So *you're* doing it?" Todd cried to Patrick. "You're giving my sister the worms?"

"Huh? Worms?" Patrick's mouth dropped open. He held a large sheet of paper in his hand. Todd saw him slip the sheet of paper behind his back.

"Yeah. Worms," Todd repeated, snarling the words. "I heard what you said, Patrick."

"Patrick isn't giving me worms," Regina broke in. "What is your problem, Todd? Why would I want worms?"

"That's where you're getting them!" Todd insisted. "I heard you! I heard the whole thing!"

The three of them exchanged bewildered glances.

"I'm not into worms any more," Patrick said. "I tossed all my worms into my dad's garden."

"Liar," Todd accused in a low voice.

"No. It's true. I helped him," Beth said.

"I got bored with them. I don't collect them any more," Patrick told him. "I'm into comic strips now."

"Huh? Comic strips?" Todd stared suspiciously at Patrick.

The two girls began to grin.

"Yeah. I'm drawing comic strips," Patrick said. "I'm a pretty good artist."

He's just trying to confuse me, Todd thought angrily.

"Patrick—give me a break," Todd muttered. "You're a really bad liar. I *heard* what you were saying, and—"

With a quick move, Todd reached out and grabbed the sheet of paper from behind Patrick's back.

"Hey—give that back!" Patrick reached for it. But Todd swung it out of his reach.

"Huh? It's a comic strip!" Todd exclaimed. He raised it closer to his face and started to read it.

THE ADVENTURES OF TODD THE WORM

That was the title in big, block, super-hero-type letters.

And in the first panel, there stood a smiling worm. With wavy brown hair. Wearing a silver-and-black Raiders cap.

"Todd the Worm?" Todd cried weakly, staring at the comic strip in disbelief.

The three of them burst out laughing.

"That's what we were laughing about," Regina told him, shaking her head. "Patrick can draw pretty well—can't he?"

Todd didn't reply. He scowled at the comic strip.

Todd the Worm. A worm in a Raiders cap.

Patrick thinks he's so funny, Todd thought bitterly. "Ha-ha. Remind me to laugh some-time," he murmured sarcastically. He handed the sheet of paper back to Patrick.

The bell on the side of the building rang loudly above their heads. Todd covered his ears. Every-one in the playground started running to the door.

Beth and Regina jogged ahead of Todd.

"So what about the worm in my sandwich?" he called to his sister, hurrying to catch up. He grabbed her by the shoulder and spun her around. "What about the worm?"

"Todd—let go!" She spun out of his grasp. "What worm? Are you still carrying on about breakfast?"

"No. Lunch," Todd shouted furiously. "You know what I'm talking about, Reggie. Don't pretend."

She shook her head. "No, I really don't, Todd." She turned to the door. "We're going to be late."

"You put the worm in my sandwich!" he screamed, his eyes locked on hers.

She made a disgusted face. "Yuck! In your sandwich?" She seemed really shocked. "That's disgusting!"

"Regina—"

"You didn't *eat* it, did you?" she asked, covering her mouth in horror.

"Uh . . . no. No way!" Todd lied.

"Ugh! I'm going to be sick!" Regina cried. She turned and, still covering her mouth, ran into the building.

Todd stared after her. She seemed totally shocked, he realized.

Is it possible that Regina didn't do it?

Is it possible?

But then, if Regina didn't do it—*what does that mean*?

"Aren't you sick of worms? Why are we digging up more worms?" Danny demanded.

Todd dug his shovel into the soft mud behind second base. "I need more," he murmured. He pulled up a long, brown one. It wriggled between his fingers. "Move the bucket over, Danny."

Danny obediently held the bucket closer. Todd dropped the worm into it and bent to dig up more. "My worms are all disappearing," he said softly, concentrating on his work. "They're escaping, I guess. So I need more."

"But they *can't* escape," Danny insisted.

Todd dropped a short, fat one into the bucket.

They both heard the rumbling sound at the same time.

The ground behind second base trembled.

Danny's eyes grew wide with fright. "Todd— another earthquake?"

Todd tilted his head as he listened. He dropped

the shovel and placed both hands flat on the ground. "It—it's shaking a little," he reported.

"We've got to go!" Danny cried, climbing to his feet. "We've got to tell someone."

"Nobody ever believes us," Todd replied, not moving from the ground. "And, look—the rest of the playground doesn't seem to be shaking at all."

The mud made a soft cracking sound as it trembled.

Todd jumped to his feet and grabbed the bucket.

"Maybe we should find another place to get worms," Danny suggested, backing away from the spot, his eyes on the shaking ground.

"But this is the best spot!" Todd replied.

"Maybe it's a sinkhole!" Danny declared as they hurried off the playground. "Did you see that sinkhole on the news? A big hole just opened up in somebody's back garden. And it grew bigger and bigger, and people fell in it and were swallowed up."

"Stop trying to scare me," Todd told his friend. "I've got enough problems without worrying about sinkholes!"

When he arrived at school on Friday morning, Todd found three worms wriggling around in his backpack. He calmly carried them out to the front of the school and deposited them in the dirt

81

under the long hedge that lined the building.

I'm going to stay calm, he decided.

They're only worms, after all. And I like worms. I collect worms. I'm a worm expert.

He returned to the building, frowning fretfully.

If I'm such an expert, he asked himself, why can't I explain how the worms are following me everywhere?

When he took out his maths notebook an hour later, he found a mass of long purple worms crawling around near the binding and between the pages.

The kids sitting near him saw them and started pointing and screaming.

"Todd," Mr Hargrove, the maths teacher, said sternly, "I think we saw enough of your worms at the Science Expo. I know you're attached to them. But do you have to bring them to maths class?"

Everyone laughed. Todd could feel his face growing hot.

"Todd's saving them for lunch!" Danny exclaimed from two rows behind him.

Everyone laughed even louder.

Thanks a bunch, Danny, Todd thought angrily. He scooped the worms up, carried them to the window, and lowered them to the ground.

Later, in the lunchroom, Todd unwrapped his

sandwich carefully. Peanut butter and jam again.

Danny leaned across the table, staring hard at the sandwich.

"Go ahead. Open it," he murmured.

Todd hesitated, gripping the sandwich in both hands.

How many worms would be crawling through the peanut butter this time? Two? Three? *Ten?*

"Go ahead," Danny urged. "What are you waiting for?"

Todd took a deep breath and held it. Then he slowly pulled apart the two slices of bread.

"No worm!" Todd declared.

Both boys let out long sighs of relief.

Danny sank back into his seat and picked up what was left of his ham sandwich.

Todd didn't eat. He stared thoughtfully at the peanut butter covered with smears of blackcurrant jam. "They're going to drive me totally crazy," he muttered.

"What?" Danny asked with a mouthful of sandwich.

"Nothing," Todd replied. His head itched. He pulled off his cap and reached up to scratch it. He expected to find a worm in his hair. But there wasn't one.

Every time he opened his book bag, he expected to find worms. Every time he ate a meal, he expected to see a worm bobbing or wriggling or crawling or swimming through his food.

He was starting to imagine worms everywhere. Everywhere.

Todd had dinner at Danny's that night. Danny's mother served fried chicken and mashed potatoes. Then she and Danny's father argued all through dinner about where to go on holiday, and whether or not they should save the money and buy a couch instead.

Danny seemed really embarrassed about his parents' loud arguing.

But Todd didn't mind at all. He was so happy to relax and eat and not worry about finding any long, purple worms on his plate or in his glass.

He and Danny went up to Danny's room and played video games for a few hours after dinner. Danny had a game called Worm Attack. Todd made him bury it at the back of the cupboard.

Danny's father drove Todd home at about ten. Todd's parents were already dressed for bed. "Your mum and I both had rough days," Mr Barstow explained. "We're hitting the sack early. You can stay up and watch TV or something if you want, Todd."

Todd didn't feel sleepy. So he went into the den and turned on the TV. He watched a *Star Trek* that he'd already seen.

He was yawning and feeling tired by the time the show finished at eleven. He turned off all the lights and made his way up to his room.

He realized he was feeling really good, really relaxed. I haven't thought about worms all night, he told himself happily.

He climbed out of his clothes, tossing them on to the floor, and pulled on his pyjamas. A warm, soft wind was fluttering the curtains at the window. He could see a pale half-moon in the black night-time sky.

Clicking off the bedside lamp, Todd pulled back his covers and slipped into bed.

He yawned loudly and shut his eyes.

Tomorrow is Saturday, he thought happily. No school.

He turned on to his stomach and buried his face in the pillow.

He felt something wet and warm wriggle against his cheek.

Then he felt something moving under his chest.

"Oh!" He jerked himself upright, pulling himself up with both hands.

A long, wet worm clung to the side of his face.

He reached up and pulled it off.

He jumped out of bed. It took a short while to find the bedside lamp in the darkness. Finally, he managed to click it on.

Blinking in the light, he saw a worm stuck to the front of his pyjama top. Three long, brown worms were crawling on his sheet. Two more were stretched out on the pillow.

"No! No! Stop!"

It took Todd a while to realize that the shrill screams were coming from *him*!

"I can't take it any more!" he shrieked, losing control.

He pulled the worm off his pyjama top and tossed it on to the bed beside the others.

"Regina! Regina—you've got to stop it! You've *got* to!" Todd screamed.

He spun round when he heard footsteps at the bedroom door.

"Mum!" Todd wailed. "Mum—look!" He pointed frantically to the worms crawling on his pillow and bedsheet.

Mrs Barstow raised both hands to her cheeks in surprise.

"Mum—you've got to stop Regina!" Todd pleaded. "You've got to stop her! Look what she did! Look what she put in my bed!"

Mrs Barstow moved quickly into the room and put an arm around Todd's trembling shoulders. "But Regina isn't here, Todd," she said gently.

"Huh?" He gaped at her in shock.

"Regina is at a sleepover at Beth's," his mother explained. "Regina isn't here!"

21

"We'll have to have a long discussion about this in the morning," Mrs Barstow said, her arm still around Todd's shoulders. "Maybe your worms are escaping from the tank somehow."

"Maybe," Todd replied thoughtfully.

His mother lowered her eyes to the bed. "Yuck. Take the worms back downstairs, Todd, and I'll change the sheets."

Todd obediently lifted the worms off the sheet and pillowcase. Two of them were mashed. But the rest were wriggling and squirming.

They're taking their revenge, Todd thought with a shudder as he carried them out of the room.

Regina was right.

The worms are paying me back.

The worms dangled from his hand as he carried them down to the basement. He dropped them into the tank. Then he leaned over it, staring down into the soft, wet dirt.

Most of the worms were below the surface. But a few crawled across the top.

"Hey," Todd called down to them, lowering his face over the top of the glass aquarium. "Hey, you lot—can you hear me?"

He had never talked to his worms before. And he felt very uncomfortable talking to them now.

But he was desperate.

"Listen, you lot, I'm really sorry," Todd said, speaking softly. He didn't want his voice to carry upstairs. If his mum or dad heard him talking to the worms, they'd know he was totally Looney Tunes.

"I'm really sorry about what happened," he told them. "I mean, about cutting that one in half. It will never happen again. I promise."

Leaning over the tank, he stared down into the dirt. The worms didn't seem to be paying any attention to him. Two of them were crawling against one of the glass walls. Another was burrowing into the dirt.

"So do you think you can stop following me around?" Todd continued, giving it one last try. "I mean, I don't want to get rid of you all. I've been collecting worms for a long time. But if you keep this up, well . . . you'll all have to go."

Todd lifted his head out and stood up straight. I can't believe I just did that, he thought.

Maybe I *am* totally nuts.

He glanced quickly around the basement, expecting Regina and his parents to pop out from behind the boiler, crying, "April fool!"

But no one else was down there. Luckily, no one had seen him actually pleading with the worms!

Feeling really foolish and confused, Todd trudged back up to his room. His mother was waiting for him in the hall outside his room. "What took so long?"

"Nothing," Todd muttered, feeling himself blush.

She swept a hand through his wavy, dark hair. "I never get to see your hair," she said, smiling. "It's always under that awful cap."

"Yeah. I know," Todd yawned.

"Go and change your pyjamas," she instructed him. "Those have worm juice all over them. I'll run you a hot bath."

"No. No bath," Todd said sharply. "I'm too tired."

"You don't want a bath after rolling around on worms?" Mrs Barstow demanded.

"Tomorrow. Okay?" he pleaded.

"Okay," she agreed. "But change your pyjamas. Good night."

Todd watched her make her way downstairs. Then he returned to his room and changed into clean pyjamas. He inspected the bed carefully, even though the sheets were new. Then he examined the pillow.

When he was certain there were no worms, he turned off the light and slipped into bed.

Lying on his back, he stared through the window at the pale half-moon—and thought about the worms.

Regina was sleeping over at Beth's—but the bed was full of worms.

How?

How were they wriggling into his backpack? Into his notebooks? Into his breakfast? His lunch?

The room began to whirl. Todd felt dizzy. So sleepy. So very sleepy . . .

But he couldn't stop puzzling about the worms. Such a mystery.

The night sky grew darker. The moon rose away from the window.

It's so late, Todd thought, and I can't get to sleep.

Maybe I do need a hot bath, he told himself, lowering his feet to the floor. Baths always relaxed him.

He crept silently out of his room and down the hall to the bathroom. He didn't want to wake his parents. Closing the bathroom door behind him, he clicked on the light. Then he turned on the water and filled the tub, making it nice and hot.

When the water was nearly up to the top, he

91

pulled off his pyjamas. Then he lowered himself into the steamy water. "Mmmmmm," he hummed aloud as he settled into it. The hot water felt so good, so soothing.

This was a good idea, he told himself, resting his head against the back of the tub. He smiled and shut his eyes. Just what I needed.

A soft splash made Todd open his eyes and glance at the tap. Had he forgotten to turn it off?

Another splash.

"Ohh." Todd let out a soft moan as a fat purple worm slid out of the tap and hit the water. "Oh, no!"

Splash.

Another worm dropped from the tap. Then two more. They hit the surface of the water and plunged to the tub bottom just past Todd's feet.

"Hey—!" He pulled his feet away and drew himself up to a sitting position. "What's going on?!"

As Todd stared in horror, brown and purple worms tumbled from the tap, three and four at a time, splashing into the bath. He raised his eyes to see more worms—sliding down the tile wall, plopping on to the water, on to his legs, on to his shoulders.

"No—!"

He struggled to climb out, trying to push himself to his feet with both hands.

But the bottom of the bath was covered with wriggling, swimming, slithering worms. And his hands kept slipping out from under him.

"Help—!"

Breathing hard, he managed to climb to his knees.

Worms clung to his back, his shoulders. He could feel them crawling over his hot, wet skin.

More worms tumbled down the wall. They seemed to be raining from the ceiling. More and more poured out of the tap.

They had turned the entire bath into a seething, wriggling sea of brown and purple.

"Help—somebody!" Todd shouted.

But the worms were pulling him now. Pulling him down.

He could feel their wet grasp, hundreds of tiny prickles, as they held him tightly and tugged him down, down, into the churning water.

They plopped on to his head. Crawled over his face. Dangled from his quivering shoulders.

Covered him. Covered him, and continued to rain down, to pour down, and pull him down with them, into the wriggling, dark sea of warm, wet worms.

22

"Please—help me!"

Todd struggled and squirmed. He twisted his body, trying to swing his arms free.

But the worms held on, forcing him down, pulling him into the slimy, brown water. And more worms rained down, curling and uncurling as they slid down the wall, dropped from the ceiling, and poured from the tap.

"Oh!"

He let out a startled cry as he tugged himself back to a sitting position. He thrashed his arms hard, sending a spray of water over the side of the bath.

He blinked. Once. Twice.

And the worms disappeared. All of them.

"Huh?" His mouth dropped open as he gazed into the bath. The ceiling light reflected in the clear water.

Hesitantly, he moved his toes. He splashed the water with both feet.

Clear. Perfectly clear and clean.

"Wow," Todd murmured, shaking his head. "Wow."

The wriggling, tumbling worms lingered in his mind. Despite the heat of the bathwater, a cold shiver ran down his body.

He climbed quickly out of the bath and wrapped a large, green bath towel around himself.

A dream. It had all been a disgusting dream.

He had fallen asleep in the bath and had dreamed up all of the worms.

He shivered again. He still felt shaky. He could still feel the itchy pinpricks all over his body.

Drying himself quickly, he let the towel slip to the floor and pulled on his pyjamas. Then, as he hurried back to his room, eager to climb under the covers—he had an idea.

He had an idea about how to solve the worm mystery.

It was so simple, he realized. Such a simple plan.

But it would tell him once and for all how the worms were escaping from their tank and getting into his things.

"Yes!" he cried in an excited whisper. "Yes!"

Finally, he had a plan. He knew exactly what to do.

It will have to wait till Sunday night, he told himself, climbing into bed and pulling up the blankets. But I'll be ready then.

Ready for anything.

Thinking about his plan, Todd fell asleep with a smile on his face.

The weekend passed slowly. Todd and Danny went to a film on Saturday. It was a comedy about space aliens trying to run a car wash. The aliens kept getting confused and washing themselves instead of cars. In the end, they blew up the whole planet.

Danny thought it was very funny. Todd thought it was stupid, but funny.

On Sunday, Regina came home from Beth's. The whole family went on a trip to visit some cousins.

"It was a no-worms weekend," Todd told Danny over the phone after dinner on Sunday evening.

"Excellent!" Danny replied enthusiastically.

"Not a single worm," Todd told him, twisting the phone cord around his wrist.

"So are you going ahead with your plan?" Danny demanded.

"Yeah. Sure," Todd said. "I have to. They just took the weekend off. For sure. Tomorrow is school. That means more worms in my backpack, in my books, in my lunch."

"Yuck," Danny murmured on the other end of the line.

"I've got to solve the mystery," Todd told him. "I've *got* to."

"Well, good luck," Danny said. "I'll meet you tomorrow morning. Outside Miss Grant's class, okay? Get there early so you can tell me how it went."

"Okay," Todd replied. "See you tomorrow." As he hung up the phone, he felt excited and nervous and eager and frightened, all at the same time.

He tried playing a Nintendo football game to pass the time. But he was so excited and nervous, he kept using the wrong fingers on the controls and the machine beat him easily.

Then he paced back and forth in his room, watching the clock slowly slide from number to number.

At ten-thirty, he and Regina said good night to their parents and returned to their rooms. Todd changed into his pyjamas, turned out the lights, then sat on the edge of his bed, waiting.

Waiting for his parents to go to bed.

He heard their door close at eleven-fifteen. Then he waited another fifteen minutes, sitting tensely in the dark, listening to the soft creaks and groans of the house, listening to the heavy silence.

A little after eleven-thirty, Todd climbed off his bed and tiptoed silently out of his room.

It's time, he told himself, creeping down the dark hall to the stairs. Time to get to the bottom of this.

Time to solve the mystery of the worms.

The basement stairs creaked loudly under Todd's bare feet. But there was nothing he could do about that.

He tried to move as silently as a mouse. He didn't want to alert anyone in his family that he was awake. He grabbed the wall and caught his balance as he started to stumble on the basement steps.

Taking a deep breath, he stopped and listened. Had anyone heard him?

Silence.

The wooden steps were steep and rickety. But Todd couldn't turn on the lights. He didn't want anyone to see him.

Not even the worms.

A pale square of light spread across the basement floor, moonlight pouring through the narrow window up near the basement ceiling. Todd stepped around the light, keeping in the dark shadows.

His heart pounded as he made his way slowly, carefully across the room. "Ow!" He let out a whispered cry as he banged his waist into the corner of the ping-pong table. He quickly covered his mouth before he could cry out again.

The pain slowly faded. Rubbing his side, Todd picked up a tall stool and carried it over to one of the concrete beams that rose from floor to ceiling.

He set the stool down slowly, carefully. Gazing around the beam, he could see the worm tank on its table. The glass tank reflected the glow of the moonlight that invaded the dark basement.

Todd lifted himself silently on to the stool. Hidden behind the square concrete beam, he could watch the worms—but they couldn't see him.

He gripped his hands around the beam and steadied himself on the tall stool. Glancing up, he saw the high window, filled with moonlight, glow like silver. The light cast eerie shadows over the entire basement.

Todd forced his breathing to slow to normal.

Got to take it easy. It may be a long wait, he told himself. I may be sitting here, watching the worm tank all night.

What did he expect to see?

He wasn't sure. But he knew something would

happen. Something would happen to explain the mystery of the worms to him.

Leaning against the beam, Todd stared at the glass aquarium tank. Were the worms plotting and planning inside? Were they deciding which ones of them would crawl upstairs and climb into Todd's things?

Todd suddenly imagined a different story. Glancing back at the silvery basement window, he imagined it opening. He imagined a dark figure sliding into the basement. Patrick. He imagined Patrick lowering himself on to the basement floor, then crossing the room to the worm tank.

He imagined Patrick pulling up worms from the tank and sneaking upstairs with them. Todd could see Patrick grinning as he dropped the worms into Todd's backpack, slipped one into the cornflakes box, hid one in Todd's trainer.

It's possible, Todd told himself, turning his attention back to the worms. It isn't a totally crazy idea. It isn't as crazy an idea as a bunch of worms planning their revenge . . .

He yawned, covering his mouth so the worms wouldn't hear.

How long will I have to sit here? he wondered. He felt a chill at the back of his neck. It was creepy down here in the dark.

What were those soft skittering sounds?

Mice?

He didn't have long to think about them. A loud *creak* behind him made Todd gasp.

He gripped the concrete beam.

The stairs began to groan.

He heard the slow thud of footsteps. Footsteps growing louder, moving down the stairs.

Todd lowered his feet to the floor. He pressed himself tightly behind the beam, trying to hide.

The stairs creaked and groaned.

The *thud* of footsteps stopped at the bottom of the steps. Todd squinted hard into the darkness.

Who was it? Who was sneaking down to the basement?

Who was sneaking down to the worm tank?

Who?

Todd gasped as the ceiling lights flickered on. It took a second or two for his eyes to adjust to the bright fluorescent light.

Then he saw the figure standing at the light switch.

"*Dad!*" Todd cried.

Mr Barstow jumped in surprise. He had a yellow bathrobe slung loosely around him. He carried one of Todd's baseball bats in both hands, raised waist high.

"Dad—what are *you* doing down here?" Todd cried shrilly.

Todd's father lowered the baseball bat. His mouth dropped open as he squinted across the room at Todd. "What are *you* doing down here?" he demanded.

"I'm . . . uh . . . watching the worms," Todd confessed.

Mr Barstow let the bat drop to the floor. It clanked noisily at his feet. He made his way quickly over to Todd, carefully stepping around the ping-pong table.

"I heard the basement steps creaking," he told Todd. "I heard a crash down here, someone banging into the ping-pong table. I—I thought it was a burglar. So I grabbed the bat and came down to investigate."

"It's just me, Dad," Todd said. "I had to find out how my worms are getting into my stuff. So I decided to watch them all night and see if—"

"I've had it with those worms!" Mr Barstow exclaimed angrily.

"But, Dad—" Todd protested.

"What's going on down there? Are you okay?" Mrs Barstow called from the top of the stairs.

"Everything's okay, dear!" Todd's father called. "It's just more worm trouble."

"Those disgusting worms again? Come up here and get back to bed," Mrs Barstow ordered. Todd could hear her padding back to her room.

"Those worms are out of here tomorrow," Mr Barstow said sternly, tightening the belt of his yellow robe.

"What?" Todd cried. "Dad, please—"

"Enough is enough, Todd. I don't understand what's been going on with your worms," his father said, frowning, resting his hands on his waist. "But I can't have you scaring everyone in the house, sneaking around in the middle of the night, sitting in the dark, staring at a tank of worms instead of getting your sleep."

"But—but—" Todd sputtered.

Mr Barstow shook his head. "My mind is made up. No discussion. The worms go. Tomorrow afternoon, take them outside and dump them all in the garden."

"But, Dad—"

Mr Barstow raised a hand for silence. "I mean it. In the garden. Tomorrow afternoon. I'm sure you can find something better to collect than worms."

He placed both hands on Todd's shoulders and marched him towards the stairs.

Todd sighed unhappily, but didn't say any more. He knew better than to argue with his father. When his dad made up his mind about something, he could be very stubborn.

Todd climbed the rest of the way to his room in silence, feeling angry and disappointed.

As he dropped on to his bed and jerked up the covers, he grumbled to himself about the most disappointing thing of all—he hadn't solved the mystery.

All that planning. All that sneaking around.

He'd had such high hopes for getting to the bottom of it once and for all.

But, no.

Not only was he about to lose all of his worms,

but now he would *never* know how the worms got into his things.

I don't *care* about those stupid worms! he told himself. I don't *care* that I have to throw them all away!

All I really care about is solving the mystery!

Angry and frustrated, Todd turned and started to punch his pillow. Hard. With both fists. Again. Again.

He didn't realize that the whole mystery would be solved—accidentally—just a few hours later.

It rained the next morning. Todd didn't even notice as he walked slowly to school. His thoughts were darker than the storm clouds over his head.

He dropped his jacket in his locker and pulled out his Trapper-Keeper. Stuffing it into his rain-drenched backpack, he spotted Danny.

As planned, Danny was waiting outside the classroom door. Waiting to hear how Todd had solved the worm mystery.

Well, I guess Danny will just have to be disappointed, too, Todd thought glumly. He straightened his Raiders cap and, hoisting his wet backpack on to his shoulders, made his way across the hall to his friend.

Danny's red hair was soaked and matted down on his head. It looked more like a helmet than hair.

Todd pushed his way through a group of laughing, shouting kids, all shaking rainwater off themselves, puddles on the hall floor at their feet.

"So? How'd it go?" Danny asked eagerly as Todd stepped up to him.

Todd started to tell his friend the bad news— but he stopped when he heard a voice he instantly recognized.

Regina!

Around the corner, out of view of the two boys, Regina and Beth were sharing a good laugh.

"So he has to dump out all those disgusting worms today!" Regina was gleefully telling Beth. "Isn't that great?"

"Fantastic!" Beth declared.

Both girls laughed.

"Todd is such an idiot!" Beth exclaimed. "Did he really think the worms were crawling upstairs on their own? Did he really think they were coming to get him?"

"Yeah. I think he did!" Regina said through her scornful laughter.

Around the corner from the two girls, Danny and Todd stood listening in shock. Neither of them moved a muscle. Todd's mouth had dropped open. He could feel his face growing red-hot.

"So today's the last day?" Beth was saying. "Did you put any worms in his stuff today?"

"Only two," Regina replied. "Mum gave him a thermos of hot vegetable soup since it's such a nasty day. I dropped one in the thermos. And I slipped one into his jacket pocket. He's on his way to school. He probably stuck his hand in and found my little surprise."

Both girls laughed again.

"And he never guessed it was you the whole time?" Beth asked Regina.

"He guessed," Regina replied. "But I'm such a good actress. I acted shocked and disgusted. Pretty soon, he didn't know *what* to think!"

They laughed some more. Then Todd heard them head the other way down the hall.

He turned to find Danny staring at him. "Todd—do you *believe* it? It was your sister the whole time!"

"I knew it," Todd lied, trying to sound casual. "I knew it was Regina."

"Well, what are you going to do?" Danny demanded, still staring at Todd.

"Get revenge, of course," Todd replied quickly.

"Revenge? How?" his friend asked.

"I'm not sure," Todd told him. "I just know it's going to take a *lot* of worms!"

109

26

The rain stopped after lunch. The heavy, dark clouds drifted away, and bright sunshine poured down from a clear blue sky.

Todd eagerly watched the weather change through the classroom windows. The sunshine filled him with hope.

This means the worms will be coming up from the ground, he thought happily. Dozens and dozens of worms.

He was desperate to get out and collect them. He was going to need a ton of worms to pay his sister back for her mean joke.

Unfortunately, just before school let out, he and Danny were caught having a glue fight during art class. Miss Travianti, the art teacher, made them both stay after school and clean up all the paintbrushes.

It was nearly four o'clock when Todd led the way to his favourite worm-collecting spot behind second base of the softball diamond. The playground was deserted. There were no other kids in sight.

Todd and Danny both carried empty coffee jars they had borrowed from the art room. Without saying a word, they bent down and set to work, pulling up long brown and purple worms, and dropping them into the jars.

"How many do we need?" Danny asked, poking in the soft mud till he found a big wet one.

"As many as we can get," Todd replied. He still hadn't figured out exactly what he was going to do to Regina. He just knew it was going to be totally amazing. And disgusting.

"You really should pay Beth back, too," Danny suggested. He dug a hole with his chubby hand and discovered three big worms tangled together.

"Yeah. You're right," Todd agreed. "We'll save some for Beth."

Todd stood up and pulled off his jacket. Even though it was late afternoon, the sun still beamed down. He was already sweating.

"Look at this one!" Danny declared. He held up a stubby pink worm.

"It's just a baby," Todd said. "Toss it in the jar, anyway. I need as many as I can get. Big or little."

Danny dropped the stubby pink worm in with the others.

Todd pulled up a really long one. He carefully brushed clumps of mud off it before dropping it in the jar. "The rain always brings up the really big ones," he told Danny.

The ground rumbled.

At first Todd didn't notice.

"Did you feel that?" Danny asked.

"Feel what?"

The ground shook again.

Todd heard a low rumbling sound, like distant thunder.

"Hey—!" Danny cried, alarmed. He stopped digging.

"That always happens," Todd told him. "No big deal. Keep digging."

Danny dug his hand back into the mud. But he jerked it out quickly when the ground shook again, harder this time. "Hey—why is this happening again?" he cried.

"I told you. It's nothing," Todd insisted.

But then a loud roar made them both cry out.

The entire playground seemed to tremble. The roar grew louder, closer.

The ground shook. Then both boys heard a cracking sound.

Todd started to his feet. But the ground shook so hard, he tumbled back down to his knees.

Craaaaaack.

"Oh, no!" Danny cried.

They both saw the dirt pull apart between them. It looked like a dark wound opening up.

Another rumble. The ground quivered and shook. The mud split open. Wider.

Wider.

And something poked up from under the ground.

At first, Todd thought it was a tree trunk.

It was dark brown like a tree trunk. And round like a tree trunk.

But it was moving too fast to be a tree, rising up from the opening in the mud.

And as the ground shook and the rumbling rose to a roar, Todd and Danny both realized that they were gaping in horror at a giant *worm*.

A worm as thick as a tree trunk.

Up, up it stretched, up from the mud, darting and dipping its enormous head.

Todd uttered a shriek of terror, and turned to run.

But his feet slipped on the wet, quivering mud. He fell forward, landing hard on his knees and elbows.

And before he could pull himself up, the enormous worm swung around him, swung around his waist, circled him, pulled itself tight.

"Ohhh!" he uttered a cry of panic.

A crazy thought burst into Todd's head: *This*

is the mother worm. She's come up to protect her babies.

And then another crazy thought: *The worms are really getting their revenge this time!*

And then he had no more time for crazy thoughts. Or any other kinds of thoughts.

Because the enormous worm was tightening itself around Todd's waist, choking off his breath, choking him, choking him.

Pulling him. Tugging him down into the mud, down into its cavernous hole.

He tried to call for help.

But no sound came out of his mouth.

He couldn't yell. He couldn't breathe.

The huge, wet worm was crushing him, crushing him as it pulled him down.

And then a dark shadow rolled over Todd. And everything went black.

Danny grabbed Todd's feet and tried to pull him free.

But the worm had wrapped itself around Todd's waist like a tight belt. Danny pulled Todd's ankles. Pulled hard.

But he couldn't free his friend.

And now the worm was disappearing back into the gaping hole in the mud, and taking Todd down with him.

And suddenly they were all covered in shadow.

"Huh?" Danny let out a startled gasp.

And raised his eyes to see what caused the shadow.

And saw the enormous robin bouncing along over the grass.

"Hey!" he frantically called out. "Regina! Beth!"

They were carrying the big papier-mâché bird home from school. He couldn't see their faces.

They were hidden on the other side of the enormous robin.

"Regina! Help us!"

And then the bird's shadow rolled over Danny and Todd.

And the worm jerked straight up. And began to tremble.

Did it see the shadow of the bird?

It jerked straight up—and let go of Todd.

Todd slid to the ground. And the quivering worm began to lower itself. Instantly, with a sickening sucking sound, it dived back into the mud.

Gasping for breath, Todd scrambled away on all fours.

The worm—it thinks Christopher Robin is a real bird! he realized.

When he glanced back, the worm had vanished back under the ground.

"Regina! Beth!" Todd and Danny shouted together.

The two girls slowly lowered their science project to the ground. "What do you want? What are you two doing here?" Regina demanded, poking her head around from the other side of the enormous robin.

"Did you see it?" Todd cried breathlessly. "Did you see the worm?"

"It was so huge!" Danny added, pulling Todd to his feet. "It was as tall as a building!"

116

"Ha-ha," Beth said sarcastically. "You guys must think we're really stupid."

"No way we're going to believe you caught a giant worm!" Regina added, shaking her head.

"You didn't see it?" Todd cried weakly. "You really didn't see it?"

"We're not making it up!" Danny shouted angrily. "It grabbed Todd. It was huge and brown and slimy! It was pulling Todd down."

"Give us a break," Beth groaned.

"Go eat worms," Regina said.

They hoisted up their giant robin and continued their slow trek towards the street.

Todd watched the bird's wide shadow roll over the grass. The shadow that had saved his life.

Then he turned to Danny with a weary shrug. "Might as well go home," he said softly. "I'm not sure I believe it myself."

Todd tossed all of his worms into the garden that afternoon. He told everyone he never wanted to see a worm again.

When Danny came over to Todd's house a few weeks later, he found Todd down in the basement, busy with a new hobby. "What are you doing?" Danny asked.

Todd's eyes remained on the fluttering

117

creature inside the glass jar on the worktable. "I'm chloroforming this butterfly," he told his friend.

"Huh? What do you mean?" Danny asked.

"I dipped a wad of cotton in chloroform and dropped it into the jar. It will kill the butterfly. Watch."

When the gold-and-black butterfly stopped fluttering, Todd carefully opened the jar. He lifted the butterfly out with long tweezers and gently spread its wings. Then he hung it on a board by sticking a long pin through its middle.

"You're collecting butterflies now?" Danny asked in surprise.

Todd nodded. "Butterflies are so gentle, so pretty," he said, concentrating on his work.

"Todd has changed a lot," Regina announced, appearing at the bottom of the stairs. "He isn't into *disgusting* any more. Now he's into things that are soft and beautiful."

"Let me show you some of my most beautiful butterfly specimens," Todd told Danny. "I have a few monarchs that will knock your eyes out."

Everyone was happy about Todd's new hobby. Especially Regina. There were no more cruel practical jokes played in the Barstow house.

Then, one night, Todd gazed up from his

worktable—and uttered a horrified cry as he saw
a big creature fluttering towards him.

An enormous butterfly.

As big as a bedsheet!

Carrying an enormous silver pin.

"What are you going to *do*?" Todd cried.

Add *more*

to your collection . . .
A chilling preview of
what's next from
R.L. Stine

Return of the Mummy

"Daddy!" Sari shrieked.

Uncle Ben lay on his back, knees raised, hands at his sides, his eyes shut. Sari and I shoved the heavy stone lid open another foot.

"Is he—? Is he—?" Sari stammered.

I pressed my hand on his chest. His heart was thumping with a steady beat. "He's breathing," I told her.

I leaned into the mummy case. "Uncle Ben? Can you hear me? Uncle Ben?"

He didn't move.

I lifted his hand and squeezed it. It felt warm, but limp. "Uncle Ben? Wake up!" I shouted.

His eyes didn't open. I lowered the hand back to the bottom of the mummy case. "He's out cold," I murmured.

Sari stood behind me, both hands pressed against her cheeks. She stared down at Uncle Ben, her eyes wide with fear. "I—I don't believe this!" she cried in a tiny voice. "Dr Fielding left Daddy here to suffocate! If we hadn't come along . . ." Her voice trailed off.

Uncle Ben let out a low groan.

Sari and I stared down at him hopefully. But he didn't open his eyes.

"We have to call the police," I told Sari. "We have to tell them about Dr Fielding."

"But we can't just leave Daddy here," Sari replied.

I started to reply—but a frightening thought burst into my mind. I felt a shudder of fear roll down my body. "Sari?" I started. "If Uncle Ben is lying in the mummy case . . . then where is the mummy?"

Her mouth dropped open. She stared back at me in stunned silence.

And then we both heard the footsteps.

Slow, scraping footsteps.

And saw the mummy stagger stiffly into the room.